AIDAN'S SHOES

written by Brent Sampson
illustrated by Bobbi Switzer

Aidan's Shoes
All Rights Reserved
Text Copyright © 2006 Outskirts Press, Inc.
Image Copyright © 2006 Outskirts Press, Inc.

Published by Outskirts Press
http://www.outskirtspress.com

ISBN-10: 1-59800-684-3
ISBN-13: 978-1-59800-684-1

Library of Congress Control Number: 2006932529

Outskirts Press and the "OP" logo are trademarks belonging to
Outskirts Press, Inc.

Printed in the United States of America

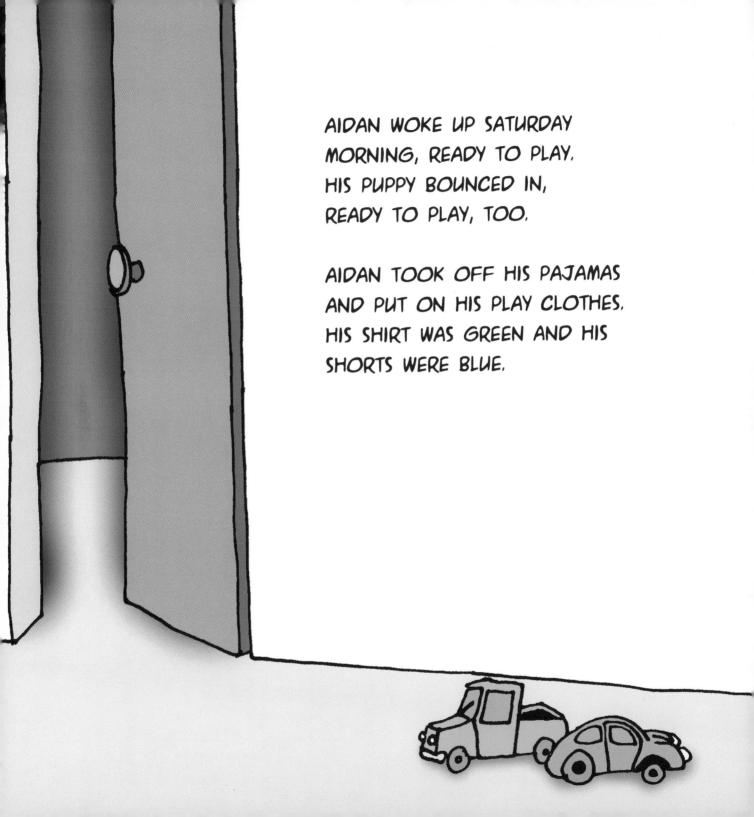

AIDAN WOKE UP SATURDAY
MORNING, READY TO PLAY,
HIS PUPPY BOUNCED IN,
READY TO PLAY, TOO.

AIDAN TOOK OFF HIS PAJAMAS
AND PUT ON HIS PLAY CLOTHES,
HIS SHIRT WAS GREEN AND HIS
SHORTS WERE BLUE,

HE RAN TO THE KITCHEN WHERE HIS
MOTHER WAS BAKING.

"GOOD MORNING, AIDAN,
ARE YOU READY TO EAT?"

"I'M READY TO PLAY," SAID AIDAN.

HIS MOTHER SMILED AND
GLANCED AT HIS FEET.

"YOU SHOULD PUT ON YOUR SHOES
BEFORE YOU GO PLAY,
YOU COULD STUB YOUR TOE OR
STEP ON A ROCK."

AIDAN LISTENED TO HIS MOTHER
AND RETURNED TO HIS ROOM,
HE LOOKED ALL AROUND
BUT FOUND ONLY ONE SOCK,

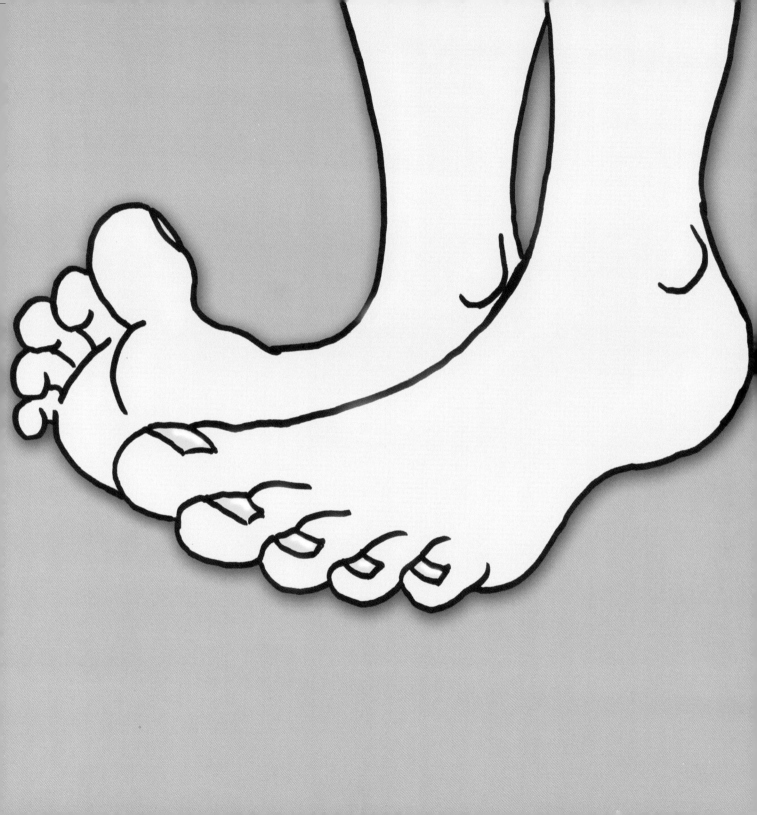

"WHERE ARE MY SHOES?" AIDAN
WONDERED OUT LOUD.

HE LOOKED AROUND AND
SCRATCHED HIS HEAD,
HE SEARCHED HIS CLOSET AND
UNDER HIS BED.

HE SAT DOWN AND TRIED TO REMEMBER THE CLUES. YESTERDAY MORNING HE HAD BOTH OF HIS SHOES.

HE RAN TO THE KITCHEN JUST LIKE TODAY. HIS PUPPY REX WAS READY TO PLAY.

"GOOD MORNING," HIS MOM SAID. "YOUR SHOES ARE UNTIED."

"I CAN'T TIE THEM," SAID AIDAN. "I'VE TRIED AND I'VE TRIED."

"HOLD EACH SHOELACE WITH BOTH OF YOUR FINGERS.
MAKE THEM AN X AND THEY'LL DO SOMETHING NEAT."

SHE CROSSED THE LACES AND MADE
TWO BOWS. THEN SHE LOOPED
THEM AROUND AND THE CHORE
WAS COMPLETE.

"THANK YOU," SAID AIDAN,
GETTING UP FROM HIS SEAT.

WITH HIS SHOES BOTH TIED,
AIDAN WAS READY TO PLAY. HE BOUNCED
OUT THE DOOR AND INTO THE SUN. "YOU
NEED YOUR LEASH," HE SAID TO HIS PUPPY.
HE COLLARED REX AND THEY
STARTED TO RUN.

THEY BRUSHED BY A
MAN WHO SAID,
"CAREFUL YOUNG FELLOW."

"I'M VERY SORRY," AIDAN
REPLIED.

"THAT'S QUITE ALRIGHT," SAID THE MAN WITH A SMILE. "BY THE WAY, DO YOU KNOW YOUR SHOE IS UNTIED?"

"OH, NO!" SAID AIDAN.
"CAN YOU TIE IT PLEASE?"

"I HAVE LOAFERS," SAID THE MAN, "MAYBE YOU SHOULD GET SOME SHOES LIKE THESE."

AIDAN CONTINUED TOWARD
THE PARK WITH REX AT HIS SIDE.
A GIRL IN A TREE SAID, "YOUR SHOES
ARE UNTIED."

"OH, NO," SAID AIDAN. "THIS ISN'T ANY FUN."
HE LOOKED DOWN AND SAW BOTH
LACES UNDONE.

"WHY DON'T YOU TIE THEM?" THE LITTLE GIRL
ASKED. "I KNOW I WOULD IF IT WERE ME."

"I DON'T KNOW HOW," SAID AIDAN.

"I'D SHOW YOU HOW IF I WEREN'T
UP IN THIS TREE."

WHEN AIDAN REACHED THE PARK
HIS FRIEND WAS RUBBING HIS SOCKS.

"WHAT HAPPENED?" ASKED AIDAN.

"I STEPPED ON SOME ROCKS. MY SHOES ARE AT
HOME AND MY FEET ARE ALL BLUE."

SO WHAT DO YOU THINK AIDAN DECIDED TO DO?

HE GAVE HIS SHOES TO CHARLIE
SO HIS FRIEND COULD PROTECT HIS FEET.

WHEN YOU GIVE OF YOURSELF YOU FEEL MORE COMPLETE.

"SO THAT'S WHERE MY SHOES WENT,"
AIDAN SAID, WITH THE MEMORIES
OF YESTERDAY STILL FRESH IN HIS HEAD.

TOYS

HE WENT TO THE KITCHEN TO TELL HIS MOTHER THE TALE,
SHE DIDN'T LOOK ANGRY AND SHE DIDN'T LOOK MAD,
BESIDE HER STOOD CHARLIE AS WELL AS HIS DAD,

"CHARLIE TOLD ME WHAT
YOU DID," AIDAN'S MOM SAID,
"IT WAS NICE OF YOU TO SHARE
WITH YOUR FRIEND, BUT CHECK WITH
ME WHEN YOU HAVE SOMETHING TO
LEND,"

"OKAY, MOM," SAID AIDAN AS HE PUT ON HIS
SHOES. EVERYONE SMILED WHEN HE TIED UP
HIS LACES.

THEN REX PRANCED IN
AND LICKED ALL THEIR FACES.

HAPPY
PUPP
FOOD

LaVergne, TN USA
04 December 2009
165778LV00002B